James Driscoll

TRAMPY'S
BONFIRE PARTY

Lesley Young

CARNIVAL

Sergeant Major had just finished his daily march around Shoe Town. He came to a stop outside his front door, then he looked over the fence into Trampy's garden, and boomed:

"Trampy! Your garden is a blooming disgrace! There are piles of rubbish everywhere. You haven't swept up your leaves.

"Even the ground is untidy," he roared. "What are all those lumps?"

Trampy looked at the lumps in amazement. "I don't know what they are," he said, scratching his head through a hole in his hat. "I've never seen them before. They've only just appeared."

"A likely tale," spluttered Sergeant Major. "Why can't you keep your garden as tidy as mine? It's the tidiest in Shoe Town!"

It was true, it was. All the flowers grew in neat rows. Weeds took one look at Sergeant Major's garden, and went next door to Trampy's.

"Never mind, Trampy," said Hector the Hedgehog, "I like your garden. It's a friendly place."

"I like it, too," said Red, the Squirrel. "There are lots of hiding places where I can store my nuts."

"I suppose it could do with a spring clean," said Trampy, "and there's a lot of rubbish in Tumbledown House that I could get rid of."

Hector and Red couldn't believe their ears, until Trampy added, "Then I can start collecting some new rubbish!"

"We'll help you gather up all the leaves," said Hector.

"But what will we do with them?" asked Trampy.

"We could store them in holes in trees, in case we need them later on," said Red.

"We could make them into a soft bed to sleep in when it's winter," said Hector.

"No, we have to get rid of them," said Trampy. "I know. We'll have a bonfire! We could even have a bonfire party!"

Trampy, Hector and Red started clearing up the leaves with rakes and brushes. Soon they had made a large pile. They found lots of things under the leaves.

"So that's where that gardening book went to," said Trampy, settling down in the sun to read it. "Let me see . . . growing pumpkins . . ."

He hadn't read much, when Trampy began to feel very hot. He shuffled off and looked back at where he had been. There was smoke coming from the ground!

Was it smoke, or was it steam? Trampy fetched a spade and began to poke at the earth where it was coming from.

"Hey! Careful up there!" came a deep voice from below.

Trampy jumped and dropped his spade. As he watched, a brown snout appeared, followed by whiskers and two small beady eyes, blinking in the sunlight.

It was a mole!

"I am sorry," said Trampy, "I didn't mean to disturb you. I didn't even know you were there."

"Don't mention it," said the mole. "Anyone who can grow potatoes like these is a friend of mine."

"Potatoes?"

"Well where did you think the steam was coming from? I've been baking one for my supper."

"But I didn't plant any potatoes," said Trampy.

"What about those old ones you found under the kitchen sink and threw out?" said Hector. "They must have put down roots and grown new ones."

"Well I never," said Trampy, "I wonder what else I've grown without knowing.

"And now we know what all those lumps are," he added. "They're mole hills."

"Can I do anything in return for your hospitality?" asked the mole. "As you can see, I enjoy cooking. Perhaps I could make you a meal – my nettle soup is quite famous."

"That sounds good," said Trampy, "and one thing I do grow very well is nettles. But what about party food? We're planning a bonfire party to burn all my rubbish."

"Baked potatoes!" said the mole. "There's nothing nicer, with soft fluffy insides, and different stuffings. I'll draw up a menu."

"Did somebody say 'party'?"
Charlie the clown appeared, as if from nowhere.

"We're having a bonfire party," said Trampy, "a rubbish-burning party."

"You can't have a bonfire – *bang!* – party without — *bang!* — fireworks," said Charlie, jumping over a Jumping Jack at his feet. "I can produce Roman candles, golden rain, Catherine wheels, silver fountains, giant rockets, big bangers . . ."

"Oh stop, Charlie," cried Hector, Red and the mole, covering their ears, "we can't stand fireworks. They terrify us!"

"I had forgotten that animals hate fireworks," said Trampy, "we can't have any fireworks in the garden."

"It did sound very good fun," he added.

"There must be a way round this," said Charlie, "but I can't think what it is."

"That's because you're a stupid clown!" roared a voice over the fence. It was Sergeant Major. "Let's ask my old friend, Sid Slipper," he boomed, "he's the wisest person in Shoe Town."

Sid Slipper was dozing in his rocking chair. Sergeant Major explained the problem to him.

"Yes," said Sid at last, "bonfires and fireworks do go together. But fireworks and animals don't go together." He paused: "But I can think of a solution. Put all the rubbish in wheelbarrows and take it to Gilda Van Der Clog's windmill. And ask Marshal the cowboy to come and see me."

The others looked at one another. Was Sid Slipper still dozing?

When the Shoe People heard about the party, they all wanted to help. They turned up at Tumbledown House with wheelbarrows and loaded them with all sorts of rubbish: leaves, logs from cut-down trees, rags, cardboard boxes, piles of newspapers.

Sergeant Major called out, "About time, too!"

"Now I've got lots of space for new piles of useful old things," said Trampy.

"Oh no," groaned Sergeant Major.

Marshal, the Shoe Town cowboy, was waiting with Sid Slipper at Gilda Van Der Clog's windmill. They all built a huge bonfire with Trampy's rubbish.

Charlie had produced a stack of fireworks.

"Tie the fireworks on to the ends of the windmill's sails," said Sid. When they were tied on, Gilda started up the wheels. Marshal shot at the fireworks with his gun and set them off. Round and round they went, whirring, flashing and exploding against the sky as they spun.

The Shoe People danced round the bonfire.

"I haven't had such a good time since my front room was flooded," said Wellington.

"And it's not over yet," said Trampy, "Let's all go back to Tumbledown House for supper."

As Sergeant Major bit into a baked potato with his favourite cheese and pickle stuffing, he said, "Do you know, Trampy, maybe those lumps in your garden were not such a bad thing after all . . ."

Carnival
An imprint of the Children's Division
of the Collins Publishing Group
8 Grafton Street, London W1X 3LA

Published by Carnival 1989

Copyright © James Driscoll 1989

ISBN 0 00 194612 9

Printed & bound in Great Britain by
PURNELL BOOK PRODUCTION LIMITED
a member of BPCC plc